This book belongs to

....

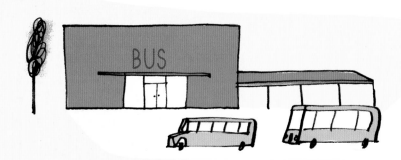

First published 2015 by Parragon Books, Ltd.
Copyright © 2020 Cottage Door Press, LLC
5005 Newport Drive, Rolling Meadows, Illinois 60008

ISBN 978-1-64638-009-1

www.cottagedoorpress.com

I Spy with My Little Eye My

VEHICLE ADVENTURE

cottage door press

Written by Steve Smallman
Illustrated by Nicola Slater

I spy with my little eye something big go swimming by. Can you spot the whale?

This package has
to get to town...
But the delivery truck
has broken down!

TOWN

SEAPORT

Find and follow the dog on every page!

This nice old car is waterproof,

Find 4 yellow umbrellas.

Where is the open manhole?

I spy with my little eye a yellow pooch that's staying dry. Can you spot the dog with the umbrella hat?

but look—
2 cars don't have a roof!

The farmer's tractor rumbles on—

Can you spy 6 silly sheep? (When you count them, don't fall asleep!)

Spot 3 pink piglets.

but where have his **3** dirt bikes gone?

Find 2 dogs playing chase!

Where is the horse hiding?

From this boat I see the trails

I spy a man in his bathtub!
Can you spot him?
Rub-a-dub-dub!

Where is my
mermaid friend?

Find a message in a bottle.

Spot 4 little orange fish.

of **4** big boats with stripy sails!

Hot-air balloons can't fly as fast

Can you see my 4 seagull friends

as those **5** jet planes whizzing past!

I spy with my little eye a bunny flying in the sky!
Can you spot the balloon shaped like a rabbit?

Find a brave little mouse!

6 yellow diggers
digging holes

Spot 3 gray wheelbarrows.

7 fire engines with screeching tires

Find the cat that's stolen my hat.

Find 3 lucky black cats.

rescue cats and
put out fires!

I spy 2 airplanes soaring high.
What else is flying in the sky?

This bicycle ride
is a disaster —

Spot an orange car.

Find 3 circus trains.

Can you see another cyclist?

9 passenger trains go so much faster!

I spy with my little eye 2 long, blue semis driving by.
Can you spot them, too?

From this submarine I spy

Spot 2 fish kissing!

Find 2 seahorses.

10 helicopters zooming by!

I spy an aardvark in a hat.
The hat is red.
Can you find that?

Can you see a green puffer fish?

"Hooray, my package
has come at last!
You didn't get
here very fast ...

You'll be much quicker going back—
I'll take you with this rocket pack!"

THE END